GOOD NIGHT, Wind

by Linda Elovitz Marshall

illustrated by Maëlle Doliveux

Holiday House New York

To my grandchildren, Gabriel, Niomi, Julia Rose, Avigail, Lyra, Talia, Leah, Noa, Baruch, Ezra, Aviya, Orly, Ellie, and all the other kind, understanding children (and adults) everywhere—L. E. M.

To my grandparents, Mamie & Grand-Père, Bubu, and Abuelito; and to all the other loving, patient adults—especially parents—who read children stories and help them grow to become kind and nurturing people. —M. D.

Text copyright © 2019 by Linda Elovitz Marshall
Illustrations copyright © 2019 by Maëlle Doliveux
All Rights Reserved

HOLIDAY HOUSE is registered in the U.S. Patent and Trademark Office.

Printed and bound in September 2018 at Hong Kong Graphics Ltd., China.
www.holidayhouse.com
First Edition
3 5 7 9 10 8 6 4 2
Library of Congress Cataloging-in-Publication Data
Names: Marshall, Linda Elovitz, author. | Doliveux, Maëlle, illustrator.
Title: Good night, Wind / by Linda Elovitz Marshall ; Illustrated by Maëlle Doliveux.
Description: First edition. | New York : Holiday House, [2019]
Summary: After working hard through the fall and winter, Wind is ready
for a nap but after being turned away time and again he becomes angry.
Identifiers: LCCN 2017024830 | ISBN 9780823437887 (hardcover)
Subjects: | CYAC: Winds—Fiction. | Naps (Sleep)—Fiction.
Classification: LCC PZ7.M35672453 Goo 2019 | DDC [E]—dc23
LC record available at https://lccn.loc.gov/2017024830

R0456439081

AUTHOR'S NOTE

This story was inspired by "Der Vint, Vos Iz Geven In Kas"
("The Wind Who Got Angry"), a tale by Moyshe Kulbak first published in 1921
in what is now Vilnius, Lithuania, under the auspices of *Der Tsentraler Shul-organizatsye*
(The Central School Organization). "Der Vint, Vos Iz Geven In Kas" is available
for online viewing through the National Yiddish Book Center archive at
https://ia801406.us.archive.org/29/items/nybc213470/nybc213470.pdf.
The author would like to thank YIVO and, most especially, Miriam Udel, Ph.D. and
Professor of Yiddish Language, Literature, and Culture at Emory University, for translating
the original publication from Yiddish to English, and for introducing her to this beautiful story.
The author is also grateful to the town of Stockbridge, Mass., for preserving the
Ice Glen Trail and the wonderment of ice caves.

Winter Wind worked hard all season long,
blowing away leaves,
preparing trees for coats of snow and ice.

Wind blasted snow across fields and roads,
sculpting drifts for children to play in.

Whooosh!

Now wintertime was almost over.
The tired Wind shuffled into town,
searching for a place to rest.

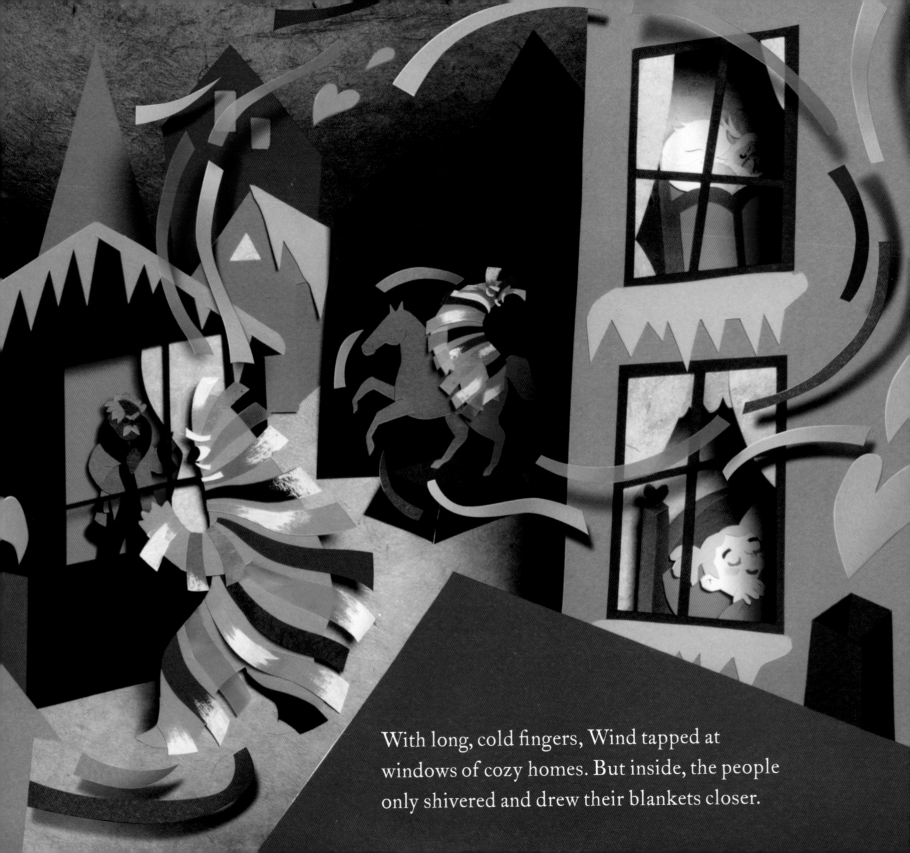

With long, cold fingers, Wind tapped at windows of cozy homes. But inside, the people only shivered and drew their blankets closer.

So Winter Wind nestled into a chimney . . .

until warm spring breezes chased it away.

Winter Wind huffed off to a
field, settled under a tree, and tried to sleep.

"YOUCH!" grumbled the tree.
"Something icy is freezing my roots!"

"Don't be angry, Tree. It's me, Wind.
Remember when I blew away your
leaves, getting you ready for winter?
I'm old now, tired, and in need
of a place to rest."

"I, too, am tired," the tree replied.
"It's been a long, cold season. And if I don't
take care of my roots, I may not live through spring.
I cannot help you, Wind. Down the road is a big rock.
Perhaps you can rest there."

Winter Wind drifted toward the big rock, lay down . . .
and rested.

"YIKES!" shrieked the rock.

"Who's lying on me?"

"Just me." Winter Wind sighed. "An old, wandering wind searching for a place to rest."

"What?" exclaimed the rock. "You can't just throw yourself on someone like that. You need to ask permission. As for me, I'm cold and dry, ready to crack, and you come along and plop yourself on me. Off with you!"

Winter Wind pushed off, trudging along the road.

When, at last, a country inn appeared,
Wind blew open the door and— *whoosh!*—
swept inside.

"OUT!" shouted the innkeeper.
She slammed the door shut.

Angry, Winter Wind blasted out across the fields,
crying like a child, howling like a dog,
wailing like a cat.

With sleeves rolled and feet stomping,
Wind whipped up a whistling, screeching blizzard.

"Take THAT!" shrieked Wind.

"And THAT!"

"And THAT!"

Snow hurtled to the ground and gusted back to the sky,

whirling in huge white sheets.

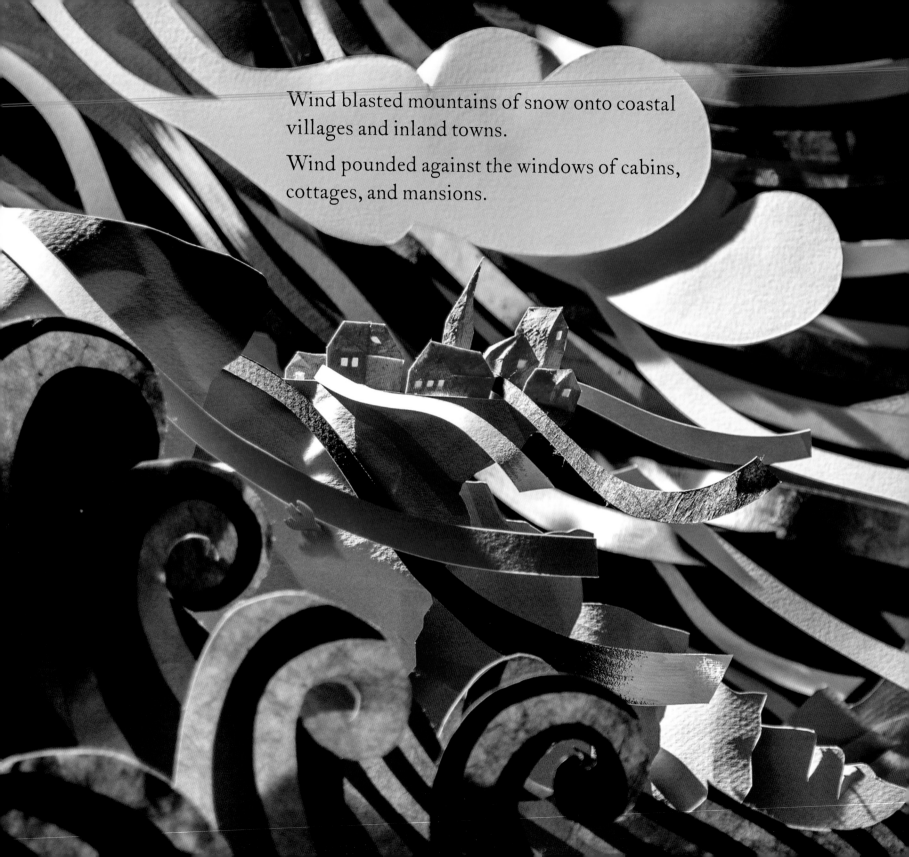

Wind blasted mountains of snow onto coastal villages and inland towns.

Wind pounded against the windows of cabins, cottages, and mansions.

Shutters closed, doors slammed.
All around, darkness fell.

But not a soul could sleep.

In a small mountain cabin, a frightened little boy cried and cried. His sister wrapped herself in a blanket, took a deep breath, and threw open the door.

"Wind," she called. "You're scaring my little brother! Stop pounding on our windows!"

Winter Wind heard, felt sorry for the girl and her brother,
and stopped pounding on the windows.

Instead, Wind howled into the chimney.

The little boy cried louder.
His sister ran to the fireplace,
peered into the chimney,
and shouted,
"STOP!"

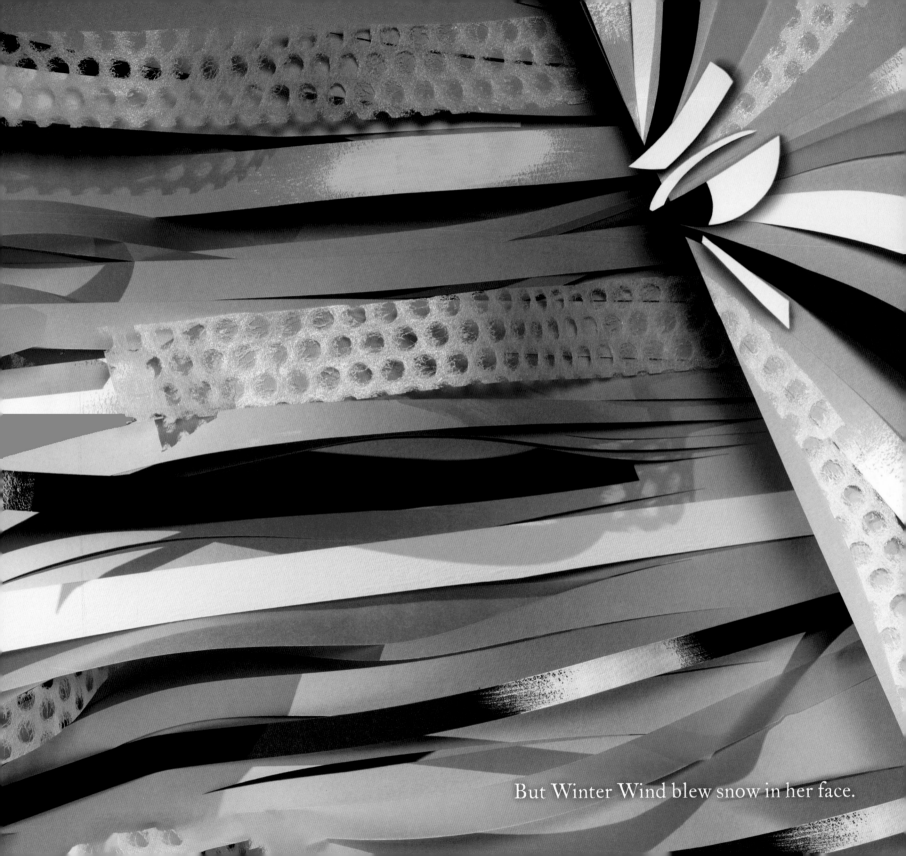

But Winter Wind blew snow in her face.

"Wind is acting like a tired, angry baby," the girl
told her brother.

The little boy wiped his eyes
and asked, "Maybe Wind needs a nap?"

His sister smiled. "Good idea," she said.
"I know just the place."

They put on coats and went outside.
"Come, Wind," the girl said. "We know
where you can rest."
Hearing this, Winter Wind grew quieter.
The snow stopped falling.

The children led Wind to a cave. Inside,
the little girl piled leaves to make a bed.

"Leaves are nice for sleeping on," she said.

"And for jumping in," the little boy added.
"Thank you for blowing them from the trees."

"And for making snowdrifts," said his sister.

Winter Wind smiled and, like a tired
baby, curled up to sleep.

"Good night, Wind," said the girl.

"Sleep tight," said her brother.

Spring passed.
Summer arrived.
The days grew long.
When it was too hot to play outside,
the girl and her brother
visited the cool cave
to check
on their friend.

Fall returned.
Winter Wind awoke.
Feeling fresh and young again,
Wind blew away leaves,
preparing trees for ice and snow.

And when winter came,
Wind blasted snow across fields and roads,
sculpting drifts for children to play in.

Whooosh!